A NEW HOUSE
FOR THE MORRISONS

BY PENNY CARTER

VIKING

VIKING
Published by the Penguin Group
Penguin Books USA Inc., 375 Hudson Street, New York, New York 10014, U.S.A.
Penguin Books Ltd, 27 Wrights Lane, London W8 5TZ, England
Penguin Books Australia Ltd, Ringwood, Victoria, Australia
Penguin Books Canada Ltd, 10 Alcorn Avenue, Toronto, Ontario, Canada M4V 3B2
Penguin Books (N.Z.) Ltd, 182–190 Wairau Road, Auckland 10, New Zealand

Penguin Books Ltd, Registered Offices: Harmondsworth, Middlesex, England

First published in 1993 by Viking, a division of Penguin Books USA Inc.

1   3   5   7   9   10   8   6   4   2

Library of Congress Cataloging-in-Publication Data
Carter, Penny. A new house for the Morrisons / by Penny Carter.   p.   cm.
Summary: Mr. Sharkey, a flashy real estate agent, shows the
Morrisons many different houses, but none seems to suit them.
I S B N   0 · 6 7 0 · 8 4 5 6 7 · 1
[1. House buying—Fiction. 2. Moving, Household—Fiction.] I. Title.
PZ7.C2477Ne 1993 [E]—dc20   93-12463 CIP AC

Printed in Singapore   Set in 18 point ITC Weidemann Medium

To Robin

Mr. and Mrs. Morrison were tired of their house.

"It's too plain," said Mrs. Morrison.
"There's too much grass to cut," said Mr. Morrison.

"I like it," Albert said to himself.

"Mr. Sharkey can help us," Mr. Morrison said.
"Oh well," Albert thought. "This might be fun."

"I will sell you a fabulous new home," said Mr. Sharkey.

Away they went in Mr. Sharkey's big car.

"No," said Mr. Morrison. "This one is too small."

"No, no," Mrs. Morrison said. "This one is too large."

"This house is too new," said Mr. Morrison.

"And this one is too old," said Mrs. Morrison.

"The neighbors must not be very friendly here,"
Mr. Morrison said.

"The neighbors are friendly here," said Mr. Sharkey.
"But there are too many of them," Mrs. Morrison replied.

"There are no neighbors here," said Mr. Sharkey.
"But there are too many bugs," answered Mr. Morrison.

"No, no, no!" Mr. Morrison said. "Too much water."

Mr. Sharkey showed many houses to the Morrisons,

but they did not like any of them.

"Stop!" cried Mrs. Morrison. "I like that house!"

"Such a nice simple house!" Mrs. Morrison said.
"We could paint it many colors."

"Such a big lawn!" Mr. Morrison added.
"We could plant a nice garden."

"But this is your old house!" howled Mr. Sharkey.

"Well," said Mrs. Morrison,
"it is the one we like the best."

Mr. Sharkey drove away, and the Morrisons
went back to their house, happy at last.

E
C

Carter, Penny.

A new house for the
Morrisons.

$12.99

DATE			

BAKER & TAYLOR BOOKS